J110,773
fa

Text copyright © 1999 by Hiawyn Oram. Illustrations copyright © 1999 by Frédéric Joos

The rights of Hiawyn Oram and Frédéric Joos to be identified as the author and illustrator of this
work have been asserted by them in accordance with the Copyright, Designs and Patents Act, 1988.
First published in Great Britain in 1999 by Andersen Press Ltd., 20 Vauxhall Bridge Road,
London SW1V 2SA. Published in Australia by Random House Australia Pty.,
20 Alfred Street, Milsons Point, Sydney, NSW 2061. All rights reserved.
Colour separated in Italy by Fotoriproduzioni Grafiche, Verona.
Printed and bound in Italy by Grafiche AZ, Verona.

10   9   8   7   6   5   4   3   2   1

British Library Cataloguing in Publication Data available.

ISBN 0 86264 868 8

This book has been printed on acid-free paper

All-Better Bears

written by Hiawyn Oram
with pictures by Frédéric Joos

Ⓐ

Andersen Press
London

Baby Bear was playing on the floor . . .

and hit her head on the table.

"Never mind," said Big Bear. "I'll kiss it better."

Baby Bear was standing on a stool,
reaching for the highest shelf . . .

and slipped and bumped herself badly.

"Never mind," said Big Bear. "I'll kiss it better."

Baby Bear was playing in the playground.

Her best friend didn't want to be
her best friend anymore . . .

and her second best friend definitely didn't want
to be her second best friend anymore.

"Not a good day," sighed Baby Bear that night.

"Never mind," said Big Bear. "I'll kiss it better."

And the next day things did seem better.
Baby Bear made a new best friend . . .

and made her old best friend
her new second best friend.

But when she went home to tell Big Bear,
Big Bear was slumped on the sofa reading a letter.

"Is it bad news?" whispered Baby Bear.
"Very bad," sighed Big Bear.
"What? All over bad?" said Baby Bear.
"All over," said Big Bear.

"Never mind," said Baby Bear. "I'll kiss it better."
So Baby Bear kissed Big Bear's tum and Big Bear's
nose . . .

and Big Bear from Big Bear's top . . .

to Big Bear's toes . . .

and Big Bear
where it tickled . . .

and Big Bear where it didn't . . .

and Big Bear all over, all over and over
until Big Bear beamed and Big Bear laughed
and Big Bear cried, "Stop, Baby Bear, stop!
Though the bad news still isn't good,
it doesn't seem half so bad!"

"That's only because I forgot something!" cried Baby
Bear jumping up and running out of the room . . .

"...THE PLASTERS!"

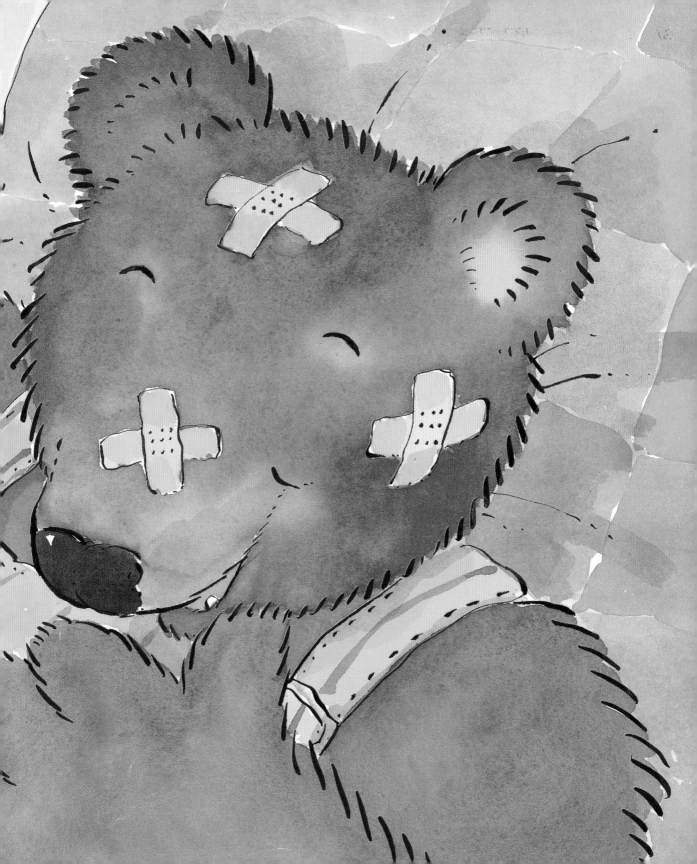